LITE CAMERA FICTION

Lite Stories from the Heart

notionpress.com

LITE CAMERA FICTION

Lite Stories from the Heart

Chhotoo Ghadge

notionpress.com

Notion Press

Old No. 38, New No. 6

McNichols Road, Chetpet

Chennai - 600 031

First Published by Notion Press 2016

ISBN 978-93-5206-909-5

Dedication

This book is dedicated to my father Harishchandra Ghadge.

Unfortunately, he left this mortal world early. His brief association with me however, has left a huge impact on me. This book would not have been possible without him.

My talented brothers Rajeev Ghadge and Vinay Ghadge were great influences in my life. We enjoyed a shared passion for films – talking movies, walking movies and eating movies when we were together. This is also one of the reasons why the title of the book is 'Lite, Camera, and Fiction!'

Had it not been for my dear friend Rini Bhaumik, this book would not have been possible. She has often suggested that I publish a book. So Rini Bhaumik, this is your book and not mine.

So when a dear friend of mine, Pallavi Kheria, said, "Chhotoo, you should publish a book, it will be a best seller," I took it seriously.

Had it not been for my dearest friend Elina D'Silva, I would not have written a single Facebook post. Every time I wrote a post, I would eagerly wait for her comments. I used to be on cloud nine whenever she appreciated them.

My mother, sister, wife, and my son are pillars of strength for me. In fact, I have written the maximum number of posts on my relationships with them.

Last but not the least, I would like to thank the Almighty, who woke me up every day without fail,to say, "Chhotoo, here is a topic, now post it on Facebook." There are many conversations with GOD which I have included in this collection of short anecdotes and stories.

CONTENTS

Chapter 1: Husband-Wife Conversation

Chapter 2: Relationship with Son

Chapter 3: Spirituality

Chapter 4: Movies

Chapter 5: Indo-Pak

Chapter 6: Short Stories

Chapter 7: General

CHAPTER 1

HUSBAND-WIFE CONVERSATION

1

Spreading Happiness, My Motto

A few days ago, I was writing till 3 am in the morning. Finally when I slept, I was surrounded by sheets of papers, magazines, laptop, laptop charger, etc.

Cut to morning:

Wife (almost shouting): What is this Chaitanya? (She does not like my name 'Chhotoo' and hence Chaitanya.)

Wife: There is a mess out here. It hardly takes a minute to arrange papers, blah blah blah…

After sometime, her 'MILYtant' activities miraculously stopped. Curious to know why, I opened my eyes. She was reading one of the papers.

Me: What happened? Why have the guns suddenly fallen silent? What are you reading?

Wife showed the paper which read:

'I Dedicate this book to my wife who….'

Wife: So finally, you have decided to write a book.

Me: I don't know about that, but one thing is sure…

Wife: What?

Me: I want to become Hrishikesh Mukherjee of Facebook and spread…

Wife: Spread… What?

Me: ANAND!

'Ruthi Raate,

Ruthi Hui Raato Ko Manaaya Kabhi

Tere Liye

Meethi Subah Ko Bulaaya Kabhi.'

2

Mily-Juli Sarkar

Today is 14th July.

Wife to me: Look at the weather today. It's so romantic. Don't go to office today naa.

Me: No, no! Today I have an important deliverable, cannot afford to bunk.

Wife: Hai Hai Ye Majboori

Ye Mausam Aur Ye Doori

Mujhe Pal Pal Hai Tadpaaye

Teri Do Takiyan Di Naukari Te

Mera Lakhon Ka Saawan Jaaye.

Me: What did you say? Meri Do Takiyan Di Naukari, how dare you say this? And your lakhon ka saawan?

Me: Who has written this song?

Wife: I guess, Anand Bakshi.

Me: I thought it was written by the former Comptroller and Auditor General Shri Vinod Rai!

Wife: Why do you say so?

Me: Only he can do such an evaluation. How did you come to the conclusion that my job (naukari) is Do Takiya? This is under-valuation of my job. And how can you say that your Saawan is worth a lakh (1.76 lakh crores). This is over-valuation.

Me: By the way, this Bangalore weather is always romantic. What is so special today?

Wife: Today, our coalition government (Mily-Juli Sarkar) has completed 11 years.

Me: Congrats.

3

Ruh, Aatma, Soul...

I was desperately searching for something.

Wife: What happened? What are you searching for?

Me: Keep our driving licences, Aadhar cards, pan cards in one place.

Wife: Why?

Me: Pata nahi. Any time we may be asked to prove our 'Nationality.'

Me: Also, keep our 'Sale deed agreement,' and all our agreements in one place.

Wife: Aur kuch?

Me: Also keep our marriage certificate and our son's birth certificate ready.

Wife: Ab iski kya zaroorat aa padi achanak?

Me: My dear wife, if we are not able to furnish these details then we may be arrested for 'Public Indecency.'

Me: Bring that temple to the living room. Keep a Murti of Ganesh, Rama Krishna in front.

Me: Don't keep that 'Bible,' 'Quran' in the living room.

Wife: Chhotoo, Hosh Me Aao, Is Desh Me Hame Kuch Nahi Ho Sakta.

Me: Why do you say so?

Wife: Kyu Ke Hum Hindu Hai. Majority hai hamaari.

Me: My dear wife. 'We are not the body but soul.' Hindu, Muslim, Sikh...these are just bodily (Chamdi) designations.

Soul, Rooh, Aatma hankers for Love.

'Pyaar ko Pyaar Hi Rahane Do koi Naam Naa Do...' Please.

Hamne Dekhi hai...

'Pyaar Koi Bol Nahin, Pyaar Aawaaz Nahin

Ek Khaamoshi Hai Sunati Hai Kahaa Karati Hai

Naa Ye Bujhati Hai Naa Rukati Hai Naa thahari Hai Kahin

Noor Ki Boond Hai Sadiyon Se Bahaa Karati Hai

Sirf Ehasaas Hai Ye, Ruh Se Mahsus Karo

Pyaar Ko Pyaar Hi Rahne Do, Koi Naam Naa.'

4

Pleasant Surprise

Thaka Hara, I returned home from office on Friday.

Wife: Chhotoo, I have a pleasant surprise for you, guess what it is?

Me: I am too tired to guess, tum hi bata do.

Wife: Guess, guess...

Me: Krish -2?

Wife: Paagal ho gaye kya?

Wife: Bought a Polo t-shirt and a pair of jeans for you.

Me: Iski kya jarurat thi? You should have checked with me before spending.

Wife: You are so boring.

I switched on my laptop. Checked some data, did one analysis.

Wife: What are you checking on your laptop?

Me: My dear wife, I am an Analyst first, husband next. As Analysts, we are trained to see a trend in the data we have. Samjhe?

Me: And according to earlier data and trends, whenever you

bought t-shirts and trousers for me, I had to spend four times more on apparel for you. I can see a clear trend in this. (95 out of 100 times you have done it, so I am 95% confident). Last time you asked me colour my hair, and according to the trend, I will have to spend on your hair treatment as well.

Wife: I have sent you a link; just check kahi wo junk me to nahi chala gaya.

I checked my inbox. There was this email from some Javed-Habib about a discount being offered for his 'hair-a-tangez karnaame.'

Moral of the story:'Beware of the so-called pleasant surprises.'

5

Yeh Kya Hua, Kaise Hua...

Tomorrow (29th June) is my wife's birthday. Before our marriage, I used to tell my wife:

"Your parents are bad planners. How can I celebrate your birthday in the last week of the month? I am not sure whether Bill Gates can do it. My brother's and sister's birthdays fall in the first week of month. In fact, my birthday falls on 8th January." "ISKO BOLTE HAI PLANNING!"

My dear friends, nine years ago, on this very day (28th June), my father-in-law called me from the hospital:

"Congratulations, you are blessed with a baby boy."

I immediately rushed to the ATM, entered an amount (Rs. 500), the screen showed insufficient balance. I tried again. I tried for Rs. 300. Armed with Rs. 300 I went to Dadar from Ambernath. I reached the hospital and this is how my wife greeted me:

Wife: Isko Bolte Hai Planning. Yehi kaha Tha Naa Tumne.

Me: But I am still wondering...

Wife: Kya?

Me: Ye Kya Hua?

Kaisa Hua?

Most importantly

Ab Hi Kyu Hua?

Finally, the nurse came and said:

Nurse: Take a look at your son…?

My son: Ye kya hua, kaise hua ……O chhodo Ye Na Ab Socho…..

(Today, our son has entered into the double digit range. Please bless him.)

6

Lovers Can't Meet in a House

CHUK CHUK CHUK CHUK...

My in-laws are with us for a few days. My wife has given me a laundry list of instructions. Sample this:

(1) Don't talk nonsense

(2) Shave every day

(3) Cut your nails on alternate days

(4) Don't give unsolicited advice to my parents

Yesterday 11 pm

Wife: And the most important thing, Chaitanya, I won't be able to spend quality time with you. Whatever little time is available, I want to spend it with my parents. Okies. It is already getting late, ab tum so jao. Bye. Good night. Shabba Khair...

Me: Matlab....

Wife: Yes you guessed it right...

Me: 'Ab Ke Sajan Saawan Me

Aag Lagegi Badan Me

Ghata Barsegi, Magar Tarsegi Nazar

Mil Naa Sakenge, Do Man Ek Hi Aangan Me…'

Wife: Chuk Chuk Chuk…

7

Dil Ek Mandir

My wife's Mummy-Papa came to Bangalore. They stayed with us for 15 days. But in those 15 days, I learnt an important lesson. I am now questioning the very institution of marriage.

Me to wife: In these 15 days, I was minutely observing your chemistry with your parents. My dear wife, how much you love each other. But the question that is now disturbing me is, "If you were so happy with your parents, why did you get married?"

Me (again): Frankly, my love for you is a drop of water when compared to the love showered by your parents on you. It is a Samundar (Sea).

Wife: Chaitanya, you are setting an impossible benchmark. No husband in this world can match a parent's love.

Me: That is why I am asking – why did you or for that matter any girl, wants to marry in first place? In my next life, I am not going to get married. I don't want to commit this sin again.

Me (again): And moreover, ours is a love marriage. You getting married to me is akin to a bird voluntarily entering a cage.

Wife: Chaitanya, after some time we (women) begin to love this CAGE.

Listen to this song from 'Dil Ek Mandir':

पंछी से छुड़ाकर उसका घर, तुम अपने घर पर ले आये

ये प्यार का पिंजरा मन भाया, हम जी भरभर कर मुसकाये

जब प्यार हुआ इस पिंजड़े से, तुम कहने लगे आज़ाद रहो

हम कैसे भुलाये प्यार तेरा, तुम अपनी ज़ुबान से ये ना कहो

अब तुम साज हां में कोई नहीं है, हम तो तुम्हारे हो बैठे

तुम कहते हो के ऐसे प्यार को भूल जाओ, भूल जाओ

Me: From now on, whenever you feel like going to your parents' house, just book the tickets – you don't have to take my permission. Just show me the confirmed tickets. Happy Journey.

8

Kabhi Khushi Kabhi Gham

Yesterday I called my wife. "Aaj no need to prepare dinner, let's go out."

My wife and son were happy.

This is what happened when I reached home.

Wife: Which restaurant are we going to? Let's go to newly opened restaurant in Total Mall 'Purna Bramha.' You get Maharashtrian food there.

Son: No, no, I want to have pizza.

Without replying I walked into the house.

Wife: What happened?

Son: Baba aren't we going out for dinner?

Mother: Arey, you were supposed to go out for dinner, kya hua? Why is Chhotoo looking so nervous?

Wife: Let me check.

Me: Today, I gave Rs. 500 to the bus conductor, I forgot to take back the change of Rs. 420 from him.

Wife: When did you realize it?

Me: Just now, when I saw you both.

MPs/MLAs, can anyone raise this issue of "Chutta, Change, Chillar" in this session of the parliament.

This is not Agrarian Crisis but is a serious one. Why "Chutta, Change, Chillar" is out of circulation

9
Ek Hasina Thi

Me to wife: What are you searching for?

Wife: Your insurance papers.

Me: Why do you need them?

Wife: Just checking, whether you have paid the premiums on time.

Me: I think I have not paid for 'XYZ' insurance, I was supposed to pay it last month.

Wife: What? Do it immediately, transfer your money that is in my account.

Me: But why today, why now, you can do it tomorrow, weekend me kar Lena, Itni bhi kya jaldi hai?

Wife: My dear husband, you have just two minutes left in your life's account.

Me: 2 Minutes, kaise?

Wife: YOU JUST HAD MAGGI.

Me: This is not fair. 'Saath Jiyenge Saath Marenge,' didn't we promise each other? Tum bhi khaa lo.

Wife: Bye, bye… Alvida….Meet you in the next life…

'Bewafaa Yaar Ne Aisa Dhoka

Jahar Usko Diya

Ik Hasina Thi

Ik Deewaana Tha….'

10

Tujhse Naaraz Nahi Zindagi Hairaan Hu Mai

My son wanted to see 'Jurassic World' but I used my veto power and decided that we would watch 'Dil Dhadakne Do.'

While watching the movie, my son picked up a word – 'Divorce.'

Son to mother: Aai (mother in Marathi) what does 'divorce' mean?

Mother: Will tell you after the BREAK (she meant interval).

Son to me: What does 'divorce' mean?

Me: What do you want to have, popcorn or burger?

Son: Combo.

Me: Wo Rs. 470 wala dena.

We reached home, had dinner and were about to go to sleep.

Son: Baba, you didn't tell me the meaning of 'divorce.'

Me: It's time to go to sleep, will definitely tell you tomorrow.

Cut to Morning…

Wife: Krish, its 7:25! The bus will reach any moment, just pack your bag, and put your tiffin in your bag.

Wife did the final checking.

Wife: Krishu, I can't see the pocket dictionary, where have you kept it?

Krish (son): I am going through it.

Wife (shouts at him): Is this the time to read a dictionary? If you miss the bus naa, then I will not drop you at school. And what is the word that you are searching for in the dictionary?

Krish: 'Divorce.'

(There was pin drop silence.)

Me: Wait a minute; I will walk with you till the bus stop.

Wife: Oh great, then please go with him. I can complete my pending work.

Me: No, both of us will go.

Finally, the bus arrived. Wife hugged and kissed him…

They were living the moment and I was analysing the moment.

It was time to say goodbye.

Wife: Krishu, I have kept the pencil box in the right pocket and the signed letter in your moral science book.

My son looked at me and smiled.

I forgot to smile because

'Muskurao Kabhi Dar Lagta Hai

Jaise Hoton Par Karz Rakhaa Ha.'

My dear son, sorry we didn't/couldn't tell you the meaning of 'divorce.'But always remember that the dictionary meanings are not always correct, please refer to a dictionary called 'ZINDAGI,' SAB SAMAJH ME AAYEGA.

My dear son: Tere Maasoom Sawaalon Se pareshaan Hu Main O Pareshaan Hu Main…

11

Zindagi Mile Na Dubara

Aaj Mai Upar Aasmaan Neeche

Aaj Mai Aage Zamana Hai Peeche

Tell Me O Khuda Ab Mai Kya Karu

Yesterday, our landowner returned the security deposit without deducting a single naya paisa. It was a pleasant surprise for me.

Mother to my wife: What happened, why is Chhotoo so happy today?

Wife: We received the security deposit from our land owner and the 'Sone Par Suhaga' is that he gave us the entire amount.

Mother: Now, please don't spend the money on a movie. Ask your husband (her son) to take life seriously. He should start saving now. Kitna EMI hai. At least you should understand this naa?

Wife: Do you think he will listen to me?

Today, the first thing I told my wife was, "Let's go and watch the movie 'Dil Dhadakne Do.'"

Wife: Chaitanya, didn't we agree to watch only one movie a month?

Me: That's, true, but what do we do with the security deposit money?

Wife: Save money naa, you don't have to spend all the money.

Me: Ab Jyaada Khich Pich Mat Karo. Let's go and watch the movie.

Wife: And what are you going to tell your mother, where are we going?

Me: Mandir.

Me: Bahut dino se Priyanka ke Darshan Nahi Liye.

Me: My dear wife, I am following in my father's footsteps. He did not believe in saving. He led his life as if 'YEH ZINDAGI NAA MILEGI DOBAARA…'

12

Where Have You Reached?

Whenever I return home from office by bus I get a call from my wife.

Wife: Where have you reached?

Me: Electronic City.

This has been going on for the last two years.

But a few days back she was surprised.

Trin Trin.

Wife: Chaitanya (she does not like my name Chhotoo and hence Chaitanya), where have you reached?

Me: Film City.

Wife: Everyday whenever I call you, your standard reply is Electronic City,' how come it's 'Film City' today?

Me: Wo Isliye, ke, everyday whenever you call me, I am in the middle of a daydream in which I normally see servers, laptops, email being sent, pen drives, chargers... And hence the standards reply,'Electronic City.'

Wife: Okay, then why did you say 'Film City' today?

Me: Because in my daydream today I saw Deepika Padukone and hence the reply 'Film City.'

13

Honesty is the Best Policy

'Jhoot Bole Kauwa Kaate

Sach Bole Taali Pitwaae....'

Yesterday, I received a call from my wife.

Me: Ha bol, sweet and short, I am in the middle of training.

Wife: Today Krish, received applause from his fellow students and a hug from the teacher.

Me: Oh really, but why?

Wife: That Krish will tell you at home.

I was very curious to know the reason. I drove faster than I normally do. I reached home. My wife opened the door.

Me: Okay, tell me the reason.

Wife: Listen from the horse's mouth.

Krish: I was supposed to choose any two options from many options. Maths club, science club, music club, etc. I choose music and maths.

Me: That I know, but tell me why you received applause and got a hug from the teacher?

Krish: Becoz... Becoz, the teacher liked it that I told the truth. The teacher asked everyone their reason why they chose maths club.

Me: And what was your reason for choosing maths club?

Krish: I told teacher, "I have chosen maths club over other options because I AM WEAK IN MATHS, ma'am…"

And then the teacher called me and hugged me.

Krish: Then the teacher asked, "In one sentence, tell me where maths is used most?"

Krish: Most of the students said, "Engineering."

Me: And what did you say?

Krish: I said, "Ma'am, my mother once told me that maths is used everywhere."

Teacher: Can you give me an example?

Krish: In cooking, we have to measure the ingredients – then only will food become delicious. In dance, we have steps 1, 2, 3, 4, that is also maths naa…?

Krish (again): All the students started shouting "Krish Dance, Dance."

Teacher: Okay, okay. So Krish, can you come here and show us some dance steps?

Krish: Ma'am, I will do some dance steps from 'Chennai Express.'

One, Two, Three, Four get on the dance floor…

And Krish got one more 'Jaadu Ki Jhappi' from his Ma'am.

14

Scamster Father

As a father, there are many things that I could have provided my son to make him happy. But broadly, by not providing a:

(1) Ground to play [a ground big enough where he can play games like cricket, Gilli Danda, Kancha (marbles)]

(2) No grandfather (grandmother is there, but grandfather would have been "Sone Par Suhaga")

I feel I am involved in some sort of 2G scam.

The other day, my son was telling my wife that he wants a sister. So by not having a:

(3) A girl child, I am now feeling as guilty as I would if I were involved in a 3G scam. But at this stage and age, this is next to impossible. What if had baby boy again?

Also, Ramdev Baba sells 'Putrajeevak' beej and no 'Putrijeevak beej.' So, this option is also ruled out.

Now I am left with one last option:

How about adopting a girl child?I am toying with this idea but I have not disclosed this to anyone, not even to my wife. She will now get to know about this on this forum.

What do you think?

A home without a girl child is incomplete and I have realized it now. Quite late in life though… How much loss have I incurred by not having a girl child?

According to the Comptroller and Auditor General, “It is a huge loss.” It is a sum total of 3-G (Goddesses).

“No Durga. No Lakshmi. No Saraswati.”

15

Bal Kalaakar

Yesterday, while returning home from office, I boarded a bus which was crowded. I did not get a place to sit for almost three fourths of the journey. Finally the bus conductor shouted at a teenager and said something in Kannada.

The teenager said, "Uncle, be seated."

I asked the teenager, "What did the conductor say, I don't understand Kannada."

Teenager: "Sir, he said, shame on you for sitting on a seat which is reserved for senior citizens."

Me: Is this place reserved for senior citizens?

Teenager: It is written so in Kannada there.

Then I called my wife.

Me: This Sunday we are going to 'Bal Kalakaar.'

Wife: Bal Kalakaar? I did not get you.

Me: That hair specialist.

Wife: O, Javed-Habib! how come? So, finally you have decided to dye your hair?

Me: Ha, it seems that I have to do it sooner. Just give me the number, I will call and fix up the appointment.

Me to the executive: Sir, can you fix up an appointment at 1 pm this Sunday afternoon?

Executive: Uncle……

'O Aye kibala ujle baalon ko rang daalo

Ban jao gulfam

Bade Miya Deewane Aise Naa Bano

Hasina Kya Chahe, Ham se Suno…'

16

Everyday Phillum

As a cost cutting measure, the wife and I have decided to watch only one movie a month.

This for me is a real austerity.

And accordingly, our choice of movie for the month reduced to 'Bombay Velvet.'

But after having read the positive reviews of the movie 'Piku,' I was in a dilemma.

Me to wife: It seems we have to watch two movies this month.

Wife: Chhotoo, I know you more than you know yourself. You are going to say the same thing the next month too. This month, we will watch only 'Piku.'

Me: In 'Bombay Velvet,' there is a surprise element. Karan Johar is playing a negative role.

Wife: Okay, then we will watch 'Bombay Velvet.'

Me: I am told that the ace badminton player's daughter, has surprised everyone with her acting talent in 'Piku.'

Wife: Badminton player's daughter, who? Oh accha, accha, the same lady who endorsed 'infidelity.' To sidha bolo na, Deepika Padukone.

Wife: The choice is between 'Bombay Velvet' and 'Piku'?

Me: Let me tell you one thing. Watching one movie a month for me is like asking me to breathe through one nostril.

Me (again): Agar mera bas chale naa, to I will watch movies every day,

Sunday phillum

Monday Phillum

Tuesday Phillum….

17

Facebook

My wife was supposed to pay a bill with my debit card, but it was declined. She called me. It was an urgent call. She wanted to check the balance in my account.

I switched on my laptop. Logged onto the net. But instead of checking the balance in my account I started reading Facebook posts.

My wife: Kitna balance hai?

Me: Abhi aur do, tin posts bas.

Friend's bas isiko 'Maya' kehte hai.

'Justaju jisaki thi Usko to naa paaya hamne

Is Bahane Se Dekh Li Duniya Hamne.'

18

AbhiMAN

On Saturday, my wife and I fought bitterly. By the next day, i.e. Sunday, the situation improved considerably. By Tuesday, there were no traces of anger. But our Abhiman (read Ego) was very much present. Tuesday was our wedding anniversary. I was expecting her to wish me. She did not. I did not wish her either…

Then I wrote a Facebook post thinking that she would call me after reading it. Till 5 pm in the evening, there was no communication from either side. At around 5 pm, this conversation took place between my colleagues and me in our workplace.

Friend 1: Chhotoo, what gift are you buying for your wife today?

Me: No, it's been 11 years, and I have never bought a gift for her

Friend 2: I think you should give her a rose for the next 11 days

Friend 3: Take her to a nice restaurant and no KRISH please,ha!

Friend 4: Don't take her to a crowded restaurant.

I called her.

Me: Where are you?

Wife: At home.

Me: Prepare 2–3 chapattis for mother for dinner, but we are going out tonight

Wife: Aaj Achanak, on a weekday. Then she realized…O shit, today is our anniversary naa, I forgot. Then we should. Krish… we are going out for dinner…

Krish: O balle balle, Shaba Shaba.

Wife: Krish, today is our wedding anniversary

Krish: Happy anniversary, baba. So, what gift are you giving to my mother, baba?

Me: You did not know that today was our anniversary?

Wife: No, I was busy with my new job.

Me: Did you check my Facebook post?

Wife: No. Let me check?

We went out for dinner. Watched 'Bahubali.' Came back home at around 1:30 am. Slept at around 3:30 am.

There was not a trace of Abhiman left in either of us: 'Gone With The Wind.'

I would like to thank all my friends in office who made our anniversary a grand success.

Actually, the process of melting of the Ego happened at around 4 pm in the afternoon, when I asked my dear friend Stephen Samuel, a dear friend of mine this…

Me: Hey, what does the holy Bible say about the husband-wife relationship? You can tell me whenever you are free.

Friend: I can tell you right away.

We discussed the issue, we argued and that's when I decided to call my wife.

> "Implementation immediate"
>
> Friends, I am convinced that we are not here to become something. We are not here to become PM, President, King, Emperor, Rock Star, etc. We are here on this planet on a project called 'Melt Your Ego.'
>
> In the process of melting our Ego, if we become PM, President, King, Emperor, etc., then it is "Sone Par Suhaga."
>
> Otherwise this planet is not a good place to live in. It is hell.
>
> Anger leads to Abhiman. Anger does not stay for a long. But Abhimaan stays. I am finding it difficult to get rid of my Abhiman which has now become a monster.

19

A Journey From Abhimaan to Silsila

Yesterday, my wife, son and I went for a morning walk. After walking for a while, we came across a cute couple. The following is the conversation that happened between us then…

Wife: Hi Ankita, good morning!

Ankita: Oh, hi! Good morning Mily (my wife).

Her husband: O, so we are neighbours…

His wife: They stay in the next block.

Her husband: Nice to meet you.

He shook my hand and shook my wife's hand too, but the handshake lasted for more than the time taken for a normal handshake.

His wife and I, did not like this. I felt like Sanjeev Kumar of Silsila and obviously, she felt like Jaya Bacchan.

Her husband: How old is your son?

My wife: Nine years…

Her husband: Nine years! Don't tell me! You look so young!

Mere wife ke dil me 'Santoor' ki veena bajne lagi, I could guess that.

Her husband to me: By the way, what's your good name?

Me: Chhotoo.

Her husband: Chhotoo?

Me: Ha my mother calls me Chhotoo, my wife calls me Chaitanya, my close friends call me Chhots and…

His wife: And…

Me: My Facebook name is Gaur Madhav Ghadge.

His wife typed something on her smart phone.

We reached home. I immediately logged onto Facebook. There was a friend request from her. The request was sent by Ankita. I immediately accepted it and then waited for some time.

On the chat scroll bar I saw her status 'Available.' Hari Jhandi mil gayi.

She: Hi Chhots…

My heart is beating, keeps on repeating.

Me: Hi

She: I was going through your posts, you are pucca Bollywood.

Me: Ha, Bollywood runs in my blood, my father was a film distributor.

She: Mere husband ka buraa mat maanana Thoda flirt kism ke hai.

Me: (Thoda???) No issues, ab aadat ho gayi hai.

She: Tum bhi handshake kar lete. Hisaab barabar ho jaata.

Me: Nahi mai thoda reserve kisam ka hu.

She: Okay, bye. Have to go school to attend his lecture.

Me: Attend his lecture?

She: Yes my husband gives lectures in school. Today's topic is how to recognize 'Good Touch' and 'Bad Touch.' He has written so many columns on women's safety. Hypocrite hai pucca.

Me: Hmm…chalo Ankita… jao husband ke lecture par taali bajaane. Bye, see you.

After some time, at around 6:30 am:

My wife: Chaitanya, get up; it's time to go for our morning walk.

It was then I realized that it was a dream.

Wife: Kya hua?

Me: I saw a dream, at around 4:30 am.

Wife: Wow, sabere wala dream aksar sach hota hai.

Me: Tumhare muh me ghee shakkar.

(Men will always be men.)

20

Demystifying Newton's Laws of Physics

Our son Krish was crying because he did not 'allegedly' complete his homework.

Wife: Now, stop crying, stop crying…

Krish is now crying with full speed - acceleration.

Wife: I say, stop crying immediately!

Me: Kya hua?

Wife: Dekho naa, first of all he did not finish his homework and on top of that he is crying. Rukne ka naam hi nahi le raha.

Me: Do one thing. Stop this fan.

Me: Now, tell me did the fan stop immediately?

Wife: No. It will slow down and stop after a while.

Me: In the same way, Krish will also stop crying after a while. Don't expect him to stop crying immediately. This is Newton's first law.

Me: Everybody continues their state of rest or of uniform motion.

And yes, according this law, Krish soon stopped crying.

Wife: And what is the second law of motion?

Me: Acceleration is directly proportional to force and inversely proportional to the mass.

Wife: Matlab?

Me: Matlab, the more force you use he will cry with acceleration. And the smaller the child greater is the acceleration.

Wife: And what is Newton's third law of motion?

Me: If you shout at him now, when he grows up he will do the same to you. (To every action there is equal and opposite reaction.)

So, moral of the story – if he does not want to do homework, don't force him.

21

LOC – Demystifying the Complex Issue of India, Pakistan and Kashmir

On weekdays, the situation at my home is similar to the Indo-Pak issue. My wife (read Pakistani) and I (read India) are at war especially during the peak hour (7:30 am to 8:30 am).

I get up in the morning and the first thing that I do is read the newspapers. These newspapers then become LOC between my wife and me. She constantly violates this Line of Control.

Wife: Keep that newspaper (LOC) down and have tea. I am not going to heat it again and again.

Then my son (Kashmir) gets up. My wife owns a major part of this Kashmir (I call it Mily Occupied Kashmir),

Mily Occupied Kashmir: Where is my water bottle?

Wife: Uff, you have not taken the water bottle from your bag; you should have done it yesterday.

I am reading the newspaper and am very much concerned about SAARC development.

Wife: Keep that newspaper down and have tea. Chai thandi ho gayi hai.

Me: Just a sec, let me read this interesting news from Patna. Nitish Kumar is forming a party.

Wife: Patni ki khabar nahi aur chale Patna ki khabar lene***!

Then my mother enters the scene.

Mother: Kya hua, sabere sabere kyu zhagad rahe ho?

Wife: Dekho naa, instead of helping me, your son has created chaos in this room.

ME: (Almost shouting): Hey Mily! I have told you several times that it is our bilateral issue. I don't want third party mediation.

Meanwhile Chhotoo Occupied Kashmir I (read Krish), is getting ready to go to school.

The situation is calm now. There is no shelling, no shouting and I wonder if Kashmir (read Krish) is the real issue.

In the Parent-Teacher Meeting (PTM), the teacher tells my wife, "Your son (Kashmir) is disturbed. He told me that my parents (read India and Pakistan) are fighting daily. Why don't you try and sort out the issue between the two of you? It does affect his overall development. And remember, he is not Mily Occupied Krish or Chhotoo Occupied Krish, he is KRISH. And stop asking your son, 'TUM KIS KI TARAF HO.'"

('Patni ki khabar nahi aur chale Patna ki khabar lene' is the dialogue from 'Saathiya.' In fact, Gulzar won the award for the best dialogue writer for this film.)

22

Men Will Always be Men

Me to my wife: Belated Happy Women's Day!

Wife: Late as usual, any ways thanks. Der Se Sahi Yaad to kiya.

Me: Wanted to ask you something…

Wife: What?

Me: Will you marry me in the next life too?

Wife: Shaadi aur tumse? Kabhi Nahi!

Me: Thanks, just wanted to confirm it.

Men will always be men.

23

FAKE DEGREE

Yesterday I was not well.

Mother to wife: Don't allow him to go office; office will not shut down if he does not go to work. Ask him to take rest.

Wife: Let me check your temperature.

Wife: My God, Chaitanya.

Me: Kitna Hai?

Wife: 103 degrees.

Me: Oh! Yahi par bhi…

Wife: Yahan par bhi what?

Me: FAKE DEGREE.

Me: My dear wife, just as in age, 40 is the new 20, in temperature, 103 is new 99.

Zamana kafi badal gaya hai.

Lunch Time. Trin Trin…

Wife: How are you feeling now?

Me: 'Haal Chaal Theek-Thaak Hai.

Sub Kuch Theek-Thaak Hai

Kaam Thoda Hai Karna Yahan

Ab Ki Duaa Se Baaki Theek-Thaak Hai…'

Listen to this song from Mere Apne….

24

4G – Greed, Greece and Gaur

Madhav Ghadge

We were leading a very peaceful and content life. And then someone came into my life. She was Maya Memsahab. I vividly remember our first meeting in Cafe Coffee Day.

Me: Sorry, I got caught in a traffic jam.

Maya Memsahab (MM): What would you like to have?

After going through the menu, me: Ye Pachas waali Coffee dena.

MM: Tum abhi bhi pachas par atke ho. You can go for 'Tropical Spice Slush.' … Don't be so boring.

MM (again): Chhotoo, it's been a long time since you got married. Right?

Me: Ha, tomorrow is our eighth anniversary.

MM: You are earning a good salary, you should buy an almaari. It is a necessity and not luxury item,

Me: I am happy with whatever I possess. Today almaari, tomorrow something else, the list will be never ending. 'Desire is the root cause of sorrow.' I am happy, my son is happy, my wife is happy. What's your problem?

MM: But fir bhi. Think of your wife. Tomorrow gift an almaari and see happiness on your wife's face.

Me: Okay, but let this be the last time.

Since then Maya Memsahab and I started meeting frequently.

MM: Chhotoo, how long are you are going to use this public transport? Car is no longer a luxury, it has become a necessity.

I bought a Nano car (Our Khushiyon Ki Chaabi).

MM: Chhotoo, how long you are going to stay in a rented apartment? Don't you think you should have a permanent address? How long you are going to shift like a vagabond?

I bought a house.

MM: A sofa, A cupboard...

The list continues...

The other day, I was with my wife in the same CCD where I had first met Maya Memsahab.

I said "Hello." But she ignored me. She was speaking to a new customer.

Wife: Who is she?

Me: Maya Memsahab

Wife: Par tumne to uska kabhi jikra nahi kiya.

Me: She is on a mission.

Wife: What mission?

Me: To convert every city into Greece.

Wife: Which coffee do you want?

Me: Challis Wali? Tum kaunsi mangwa rahi ho?

Wife: Hmmmm, 'Tropical Spice Slush.'

Wife (again): Kya hua, tum us Maya Memsahaab ko itna gusse se kya dekh rahe ho?

Me: Listen to this song–you will know why I am angry with Maya Memsahaab. Song from Marathi classic 'Pinjra.'

'Shrote Aika Ho…

Tyaala Eka Menakechi Drishta Laagali

Kashi Nashibaana Thatta Aaj Mandali.'

25

Ardhi Poli (Half – Chapati)

Whenever I ask my mother to give 'Ardhi poli' (half chapatti), she always gives me 3/4 of a chapatti. But when I ask my wife the same, she gives me exactly half. I was about to announce the following to the world:

"Ask your mother and you shall receive more, ask your better half and you shall receive exactly half."

This empirical evidence was not enough though. I thought I should collect more evidences and accordingly, this time I asked my son to ask his mother for half a chapatti. She gave him exactly half a chapatti as well.

So, my hypothesis proved wrong. There are so many inferences that can be drawn from this simple experiment.

CHAPTER 2

RELATIONSHIP WITH SON

1

Advice to My Son

"Aa Chal Ke Tujhe
Mai Leke Chalu Ek Aise Gagan Ke Tale….."
Taali Par Khush Nahi Hona
Gaali Ko Chup-Chaap Sahnaa
Mehmaan Hai Ye Do Pal Ke
Kab Aaye Aur Kab Ye Jaaye
Mehmaan Ki Tarah
Inhe Treat Tum Karo
Inse Rishte Kabhi Naa Bane
Jaha Gam Bhi Naa Ho
Aaso Bhi Naa Ho
Bas Pyaar Hi Pyaar Pale….
Jab Gussa Tujhe Sataaye
Tu Boil Naa Hona Pyaare
Thoda Der Me Gussasa Tera

Vapour Ban Ke Ud Hi Jaaye

Jitna Bhi Mila, Usme Content Raho

Jyaada Ki Laalach Me Aatma Naa Jale

Jaha Gam Bhi Naa Ho

Aaso Bhi Naa Ho

Bas Pyaar Hi Pyaar Pale

Apna Views Rakhne Se Pehle

Dusroon Ka Views Sunle Pyaare

Paanch Ungliyaa Hoti Nahi Barabar

Ye Samajh Ke Respond karna Pyaare

AND MOST IMPORTANTLY

Tera DHARM Tujhe Accha Gar Lage

Dusron Ka DHARM Buraa Naa Lage

Koi Jor Nahi, Koi Shor Nahi

Sab Miljulke Saath Rahe

Kuch Aise Gagan Ke Tale

2

First Day of School

(1st day after looooong Holidays - Here is email exchange between parents and teachers Bollywood ishtyle).

Letter to teacher from parents:

Dear Teacher,

"School Jise Bheja Hai Bus Me

Beta/Beti Nahi Mera Dil Hai

Teacher Hamaare Humko Likhna

Kya Ye Padhne Ke Kaabil Hai"

Teacher's email to Parents

Dear Parents:

Beta Tumhaara Badmaash Hai Itna

Beti To Class Me Hi Soti

Teachers Saare Soch Rahe Hai Milkar

Kash Ye Chutti Di Nahi Hoti

Teacher's message to Son/Daughter:

"Khat Se Jee Bhartaa Nahi Ab

Parents Mile To Chain Mile

PTM Ki Date Tay Karte Hai

Kab Aaoge Email Karna"

"School Jise Bheja Hai Bus Me….."

3

Parent-Teacher Meeting

Two weeks back I had gone to attend PTM. Reluctantly though.

Class teacher: Sir, your son is very good in studies. Got A grades in almost all the subjects except mathematics.

Wife: "Krish, but you told me that you did well in the subject."

Maths teacher: He makes silly mistakes, always is in a hurry.

French teacher: All you have to do is to sit with a dunda, that's what is required.

After listening to all the complaints, we were about to leave.

It was then one of the teachers came and said,

"Sir, we were a little harsh on you. But all of us want your son to do well."

With tears in her eyes, she said. Now for next one month, we will have to be without Krish.

"Your son is gem of a person. His heart is in right place."

Me: "Ha that I know, but he is not good in maths. Ye dil wil to bus luxury hai."

Teacher: "No sir, he will rule the world, mark my words. The other day I was not well. During lunch recess while all the kids were playing, your son came and asked:

"What happened mam, are you not well, shall I get some water for you?"

Me: Hmm. Not sure how this quality will make him a ruler though.

Wife: Bilkul inpar gaya hai

Me: Madam, for your information. At one point of time we were in the business of film distribution.

Teacher: O really?

Me: And guess the name of the movie we last distributed?

Me: It was Rishi Kapoor, Tina Munim starrer movie "Bade Dil Wala."

Teacher: No wonder.

Me: Thanks, we have to go for a 2:30 movie show.

Teacher: Which movie?

Krish: Byomkesh Bakshi. Mam do you want to join us?

Teacher: Puri filmi family hai.

Me: "Koi Shaque?"

4

Common Admission Test of My Son Krish

Counsellor to wife and me:- See, we cannot directly admit your son to the third standard. But will speak to the management if they can consider this as a special case.

Counsellor: - Follow me, I will show you the school premise. In the meanwhile Krish can write these simple questions.

When we came back, we found that Krish was stuck with one problem.

Krish: - Mam I have completed the test, but I am stuck with this question about "adjective."

My wife: - Krish you don't know adjectives?

Counsellor: - Wait, I will give you an example of adjective. How is your mother? Is she "good" or… "Nice"?

Krish: - Mam, she is "beautiful." Yes, yes now I know what an adjective is.

When we came out of cabin, Krish went inside and said something to the counsellor. But from her expression I could make out that she was embarrassed.

The counsellor came out of the cabin and said:

Counsellor: - Your son came inside the cabin and do you know what he said?

Wife: - What did he say?

Counsellor: - "Mam you are so beautiful."

Counsellor: - I must say sir, you are such an introvert and your son is exactly the opposite.

Wife: - Yes my husband is very shy. Do you know that he has not proposed me as yet? Did not say "I love you as yet." Bahut sharmila hai.

Me to wife:-

"Meri Behoshi ka matlab

Ye nahi hai ke

Ke mai tumhe pyaar nahi karta

Hosh me aane do fir pyaar kar loonga."

5
विद्या विनयेन शोभते
(VIDYA VINAYENA SHOBHATE)

A friend of mine asked my Nine-year-old son:

Friend: - Do you believe in God?

Son (looking at me):- Yes.

Friend: - So, you believe in God because your father believes in God, right?

Son (again looking at me):- Yes.

Friend: - Do you like science?

Son: - Yes very much. I am "Science captain."

Friend: - Then beta, why do you believe in GOD?

Here is my advice to my son

विद्या विनयेन शोभते Vidya Vinayena Shobhate

My dear son, by all means inculcate scientific temper. I am all for it.

But always remember that the universe is made up of

(1) 70–75% dark energy

(2) 20–25% dark matter

The universe which is perceptible, known to us (stars, galaxies, people, river, trees etc)… is just 4–5%

So bend down on your knees, be humble.

Whenever you walk past a garden, river, mountain, etc., you should ask:

"Wow, Ye Kaun Chitrakar hai?"

If you are humble then more will be revealed to you. Remember, for water to flow from one place to another there should be a potential difference. Ditto for education.

विद्या विनयेन शोभते

Vidya Vinayena Shobhate

Humility adds lustre to Education.

So, continue with your scientific enquiry but at the same ask

"Ye Kaun Chitrakar Hai?"

6

Visit to Apollo Clinic

Bade Dil Waale (The Rishi Kapoor-Tina Munim starrer film. This was our last movie as a film distributor).

We were at Apollo Clinic, Bangalore. We went there to collect my blood reports and get some consultation from a diabotologist. After doing ECG, etc. we were told to meet a Dietitian.

Dietitian: - Show me your reports.

Dietitian: - Hmm, your triglycerides are on the higher side, and so is your fasting and PP sugar.

Dietitian: - You need to include more complex carbohydrates in your diet and consume less simple carbohydrates.

Krish (Son):- Very funny.

Dietitian: - What is so funny?

Krish: - You just said complex is good and simple is bad. That is why I said "Very funny."

Dietitian: - Since your father is diabetic he should reduce intake of simple carbohydrates. Simple carbohydrates "raise blood glucose levels quickly..."

Krish: - And complex?

Dietitian: - Complex carbohydrates get slowly absorbed in blood, so the blood glucose levels rise slowly.

Krish: - Just like my father and mother.

Dietitian: - How?

Krish: - My father is simple but my mother is very complex.

Krish:- Aunty, in our school, when the "Columbia Asia" people had come naa, that time also they had told the same thing. They explained the "Food Pyramid."

Dietitian: - They explained "Food Pyramid," did you tell your father/mother?

Krish: - Aiyooooo.

Dietitian: - What happened?

Krish: - If I tell my mother then I will not get junk food.

Dietitian: - What do you know about the Food Pyramid?

Krish: - The bottom of the pyramid foods are "tasty" and the top of the pyramid foods are not so tasty.

Dietitian: - Very naughty.

Dietitian: - Mr. Ghadge, no amount of tablets/insulin can become substitute for your physical activity. You should walk at least for half an hour.

Krish: - You will always find my father in bed, writing, writing, Facebooking....

Dietitian: - Then you should pull him out of the bed.

Krish: - Aiyoo he is so heavy.

Dietitian: - Did you show your ECG to the general physician?

Wife: - Yes we did, he asked us to meet the cardiologist.

Dietitian: - You better meet him.

Me:- Any issues?

Dietitian: - Nothing as such, but check with the cardiologist before you leave.

Dietitian: - And Krish, the next time call us to your school.

Krish:-But the Food Pyramid will be the same naa…

Wife: - Ok doctor, we will go and meet the cardiologist. Thanks.

The Dietitian then called "Krish."

Krish: - Did you call me Aunty?

Dietitian: - Say "Aiyoo."

Krish: - "Aiyooooo."

Receptionist: - I am sorry; the cardiologist is in a conference. I am afraid he won't come to the clinic today. Can you come on Monday?

Me:- We will come next week, on Saturday.

Receptionist: - If the general physician has asked you to meet the cardiologist then you should meet him ASAP, don't delay.

Krish: - Baba what happened to your heart?

Me:- Nothing.... My dear son.

"Jeevan Ke Din Chhote Sahi

Hum Bhi Bade Dil Waale

Kal Ki Hame Fursat Kaha

Soche Jo Hum Matwaale

Apne Yahi Chaar Pal Hai

Aage Hai Kya Kisane Jaana

Jeena Jise Aata Hai Woh

Inme Hi Mauj Manaale

Kalki Hame Furasat Kaha

Soche Jo Hum Matwaale..."

7

Andhi in Indian Constitution

Do you remember these lines from Andhi? :

Sanjeev Kumar:

"Suno Aarti Ye Jo Phulon Ki Bele Nazar Aati hai na darasal

Ye Bele Nahi Hain, Arabi Me Aayaten Likhi Hain

Ise Din Ke Waqt Dekhna Chahiye Saaf Nazar Aati Hain

Din ke waqt ye sara pani se bhara rahta hai, din ke waqt jab ye fuvvare…

On similar lines….

My son who is ten years old now, would have completed his fourteenth year when the current Lok Sabha will get dissolved.

Me:- My dear son, ye jo Bharat Ka Samvidhaan hai naa, ise apne padosi mulk Pakistan ki nazar se dekhna.

Me:- Tab pata chalega ki hamare founding fathers ne hame kitna khubsurat tohfaa diya hai (Tohfa- Indian constitution).

Son: - But baba, what explains the emergency-like situation. Are there not enough safeguards (read checks and balalances) in our constitution?

Me:-Ha bete, beech me Amavas aa jati hai (read emergency).

Son: - Baba, for how long years did the Emergency under Indira Gandhi last?

Me:- Bete Waise last time Amavas (emergency) 2 saal ki thi.

Me:- Lekin is baar…?

Son: - 5 baras lambi thi naa…

8

Chhoti si Aasha

Watching "Swades" with my son. The first question he asked me, "Baba, when will I go to US?"

Me:- Watch the entire movie and then ask me the same question again.

Son: - "Baba I want to become scientist, NASA is so nice."

Me:- Hmmm....

Dil Hai Chhota Sa

Chhoti Si Aasha

Chand Taaro Ko

Chune Ki Aasha

NASA me Scientist Banane Ki Aasha

I am curious to know whether his attraction for the US/ NASA remains at the end of the movie.

(Right now he is asking me too many questions...)

9

World-view – Through the Eyes of Other People

A few days back I watched ABCD2 and I thoroughly enjoyed the movie.

People often tell me, "Chhotoo tumhari taste ko kya ho gaya? On one hand you like movies like Shahid, Manjunath, Piku, Lunch box on the other hand you like movies like ABCD2, Happy New Year and Chennai Express. Strange taste!!!"

Let me try to explain this.

If I had watched ABCD2 alone, I would have left the theatre in two minutes.

The movie has wafer-thin story line and a bad script.

But when I watched the movie with my nine-year-old son, who enjoyed the movie so much that nowadays he does not stand, he just dances, I too enjoyed the movie.

So, I can say that I watched the movie through the eyes of my son and that's why I enjoyed the movie.

Then there were movies like Manjunath and Shahid which I watched with five people in the entire theatre (including my wife, son) and I liked them.

Once, Atal Bihari Vajpayee visited Kashmir. He famously said, "Kashmir Ko Insaaniyat Ki Nazaron Se Dekho."

Waheeda Rahman's (Julie in Guide) world becomes different when she sees the world through Raju the Guide. (No wonder she says, "Aaj Fir Jeene Ki Tammana Hai....")

On the battle of Kurukshetra, Arjuna asked Krishna, "My dear lord, please show me your universal form (Vishvaroop)."

Krishna says, "You cannot see the universal through your eyes, look at it through my eyes."

Basically what Krishna is trying to tell Arjuna?

Ye Tera Ghar Ye Mera Ghar

Kisi Ko Dekhna Ho Gar

To Pehle Aankhen Maangle

Meri Nazar Teri Nazar

Ye Ghar Bahut Haseen Hai.

CHAPTER 3

SPIRITUALITY

1

Different Paths and Their Destinations – Aandhi in My Life

Conversation with the Lord.

Me: Sirjee, I am thoroughly confused. Please enlighten me as to which is the path that leads to you. And Sirjee, please explain to me in layman's language.

Lord: Will try to explain in your ishtyle. Broadly there are two paths that lead unto me

Is Mod Par Aate Hai

Kuch 'Susta' Kadam Raste

Kuch 'Tej' Kadam Raahe

Me: Can you please elaborate?

Lord: There are those souls who try to analyse Me, My Creation. They are known as reductionists. 'Neti Neti.'(Not this, Not that) types. This is a very slow process. No matter how slow and tedious this process is, it finally leads unto me.

Me: And what about 'Tej Kadam Rahe'?

Lord: After years of enquiry and efforts, the soul finally gives up and says,'My Lord, You and Your Creation are so very complex that I give up. Now you show me the path. I surrender unto you.'

Me: You mean, blind faith, blind surrender?

Lord: No I don't say that you surrender your intelligence. I say, surrender with intelligence. Take your own time.

Lord: But even these souls fail because their faith is 'flickering.' They almost reach the destination but then it's back to square one.

IK Door Se Aati Hai

Paas Aa Ke Palati Hai types

Lord: And there are souls, who do not make an effort to reach me.

Ik Raah Akeli Si

Rukati Hai Naa Chalti Hai

Me: In Reshmi Raaho me,

Ik Raah To Woh Hogi

Tum Tak Jo Pahunchti Hai

Us Mode Se Jaate Hai.

Lord: All the best.

2

HE CAME HE WROTE AND HE LEFT

Times Then: Good morning ladies and gentlemen. Yesterday, across India, in all the places of worship, be it the Church, Temple, Mosque, Gurudwara, you name it… Someone mysteriously entered the places of worship and then HE wrote something on the Guest Register which is kept at the entrance. There is mass hysteria now.

Ladies and gentlemen, this has happened in big and small places of worship, cutting across different religions. This is unprecedented.

The Indian government has directed all the district officials to take the signed registers in their possession. The handwriting expert is going to analyse what has been written.

My reporters are present everywhere. Let me first go straight to one such place of worship.

Reporter: Arnob, I am in front of this beautiful mosque and all I can hear is the chants of 'ALLAH HU AKBAR.'

Reporter 2: I am front of ISKCON and all I can hear is 'Hare Krishna Hare Rama.'

Reporter 3: I am in front of a Gurudwara and people have flocked here since morning. They are chanting 'WAHE GURU, WAHE GURU…'

Arnob: This is a miracle. Everyone is asking, who was HE, why did HE come, what message did HE write?

Reporter: Arnob, in five minutes, government officials are going to reveal what has been written in the register.

Arnob: Ladies and gentlemen, BREAKING NEWS… Let us go straight back to Delhi where the Home Minister is addressing a press conference.

Home Minister: Good morning. We have spoken to handwriting experts all over the country and they have sent me their reports.

Home Minister: The handwriting is of ONE person. We have gone through the registers of all the places of worship (be it Temples, Gurudwaras, Mosques, Churches….), and there is only one message…And the message is….'STOP HATRED.'

'Krishna nee begane baro

Krishna nee begane baro

We need a teacher

You are the only one

Come back Rama

Come back as Allah

Come back as Anyone

I am waiting

I am waiting'

3

ART OF 'LEAVING'

'He/She is no more' is no longer shocking news for me. The news has lost its shock value.

The other day, my sister called me to give me some news. It was a weekday and I was busy with work.

Sister: Chhotoo there is bad news. Our father's sister has just passed away.

Me: O Accha Accha.

Sister: What Accha Achaa?

Me: O sorry, I mean, Bura Bura.

Sister: But she suffered a lot. Her last days were very painful, she was bedridden…

Me: Good for her that she left this mortal world.

Sister: But my worry is, how do I break this news to our mother?

Me: Was Aunty older than our mother?

Sister: What difference does it make?

Me: It does. Then our mother's reaction will be on predictable lines –"Hey Bhagwan, even the younger ones are leaving this mortal world, what sin have I committed that God has preferred her over me?"

(And you thought there is competition only to get admission to prestigious colleges! There is competition to get admission to God's kingdom too!!)Then she will pray to God, 'Bhagwan Mera Number Kab Aayega?' The other day, I took her to the 'Chikka Tirupathi' temple so that she would feel better. But there too she prayed, "God, I cannot bear this pain, let this be my last trip."

There are many courses on Art of Living. Old people like my mother who are going through pain, badly need a crash course on 'ART OF LEAVING.' And unfortunately, there are none.

There are many devotional songs which can be termed as template songs for people who are desperately waiting to leave this mortal world. This is my favourite. Listen to this song sung by Anup Jalotaji:

'Itna Tu Karna Swami Jab Pran Tan Se Nikale

Jab Kanth Pran Aaye

Koi Rog Naa Sataaye

Yam Daras Naa Dikhaaye

Jab Pran Tan Se Nikale.'

4

Temple: The Ego Service Centre

Normally, I go to the temple on weekends. But this time I went on a Wednesday.

Here is my conversation with the God.

God: Hi Chhotoo, what a pleasant surprise! I didn't expect you to come on a weekday. Anyways, bolo Banda aapki khidmat me kya seva kar sakta hai?

Me: First thing first, Sirjee, I am really sorry, this trip was so sudden and urgent that I forgot to bring fruits for you (as I normally do).

God: Koi baat nahi. I am 'Bhaav Grahi.' I take the essence of a devotee's attitude.

This private conversation lasted for about 15 minutes. I was about to leave. It was then that the Lord reminded me:

God: Chhotoo, aap kuch bhool to nahi rahe ho.

I checked my valet, spectacles and car keys.

Me: Sirjee, I don't think so.

God: Take back your 'EGO.' Kabhi Kabar is EGO Ko Servicing Ke Liye Weekdays Bhi Le Aaya Karo.

'Agar Mujhse Muhabbat Hai

Mujhe Sab Apne Gam De Do

In Aankhon Ka Har Ek Aasu

Mujhe Meri Kasam De Do...

Agar Mujhse Mohabbat hai...'

5

Agale Janam Mohe Kutta Naa Kijo

Last week, I visited a past/future life therapist's clinic.

"It will take at least 2–3 sessions to uncover your past lives. Please share everything you read/write with me. If you are on Facebook, then share your login id and password with me," she said.

Curious to know about my past/future life, I met her at her clinic yesterday.

Therapist: You must be very excited to know about your past lives, aren't you?

Me: Super-excited.

Therapist: Mr. Chhotoo Ghadge, in your past life you were a DOG.

Me: Dog?

Therapist: In the past five lives, you were a dog.

Me: Shocking.

Therapist: In fact, in the last life, you were the same dog on whom the Russian Physiologist conducted a series of experiments, famously known as the Pavlovian classical conditioning experiment.

Therapist: Mr. Chhotoo, even if I had not met you in person, just going through your Facebook pages and your Facebook posts, I would have uncovered the same.

Me: How?

Therapist: Your behaviour is so predictable, Chhotoo. And I am sorry to say, if you continue with the same behaviour, in your future life, you will be born again as a dog. And the next time, you will not be so fortunate to be Pavlov's dog.

Me: If in the past five lives I were a dog, then how come I got this human form this time?

Therapist: So that in this life 'Tum thoda sudhar jaaoge,' but you have maintained status quo.

Therapist: Your reflexes/reactions to any stimulus are no different than the Pavlovian dog. I am sorry to say that, from hunter gatherers to the present state, you have not progressed an inch. And hence, in the next life too, you will be given the dog's body.

Me: How can I reverse this?

Therapist: Whatever may be your political or religious beliefs, your reaction should not be knee-jerk. Remember, in reel life there is 'Lights, camera, action.'

Therapist: In real life it is 'Lights,' 'Camera' and then wait wait and wait. Don't jump into any hasty conclusions.

Take a deep breath. Let the cloud of anger pass and then react. May be you won't feel like reacting to the same. Don't pronounce anyone guilty before proven innocent.

Therapist: And say this prayer almost daily before waking up and going to bed.

'Agale Janam Mohe Kutta Naa Kijo.'

Me: Which one?

Therapist: Ab Jo Kiyo Ho Data

Aisa Naa Kijo

Agale Janam Mohe Kutta (dog) naa kijo.'

Therapist: Since your next life is going to be the same, I won't charge extra for predicting your future life.

6

Badmaashiya

Two years ago my son (Krish) used to regularly visit the Krishna temple. He used to play mridanga, kartal and would sit and listen to preachers who were devotees of Radha and Krishna.

Krish used to love preaching and was always on the lookout for an audience. Once, a devotee friend of mine decided to hear Krish's lecture (Katha). It was around 11 pm. Like a professional preacher, Krish started narrating Krishna's pastimes. My friend was enjoying the lecture.

All of a sudden, Krish became serious, changed the topic and said:

Krish: Prabhuji, if you do badmashi and pluck a flower and offer it to Krishna, He will not accept it.

(Vaishnava devotees addresses each other as 'Prabhuji.')

My friend: Krish Prabhu, what happened why are you saying this? Who did badmashi?

Krish: Prabhuji, my father did badmashi yesterday. And this morning, he plucked flowers to be offered to Krishna, but Krishna said, "No, no I don't want your flowers."

Friend: What badmashi did your father do Krish?

Krish: My father shouted at my mother, and this is the badmashi he did yesterday. And so God did not accept the offerings.

My friend was astonished.

Friend: Krish, see your father has to do so many things. He has to go for work and so sometimes he may get angry, otherwise he is such a sober devotee. So, you should beg forgiveness from Krishna…

Krish: Krishna cannot forgive my father. My father should say sorry to my mother then may be Krishna can forgive him.

So, even if one shouts at a fellow human being, according to my son Krish, this is badmashi and God does not approve or accept the offerings.

I think what my son was trying to say was something similar to this verse from the Bible:

'Therefore if you are presenting your offering at the altar, and there remember that your brother has something against you, leave your offering there before the altar and go; first be reconciled to your brother, and then come and present your offering…'

7

Scientific Temperament vs. Religion

A few days ago, we were discussing 'Scientific temperament vs. Religion.'

During the conversation, Lavlesh Upadhyay said a very profound thing, "Sir, main apne dharma ke khilaaf sun sakta hu." And he said this while retaining his trademark calm and composure, without a trace of anger.

Lavlesh Upadhyay is only in his mid-twenties. How many of us (including the so-called Saints and the so-called gurus) can do this?

So the next time you come upon a sadhu or a saint, just say a word or two against his/her religion and check his reaction. Sab Pata chal jaayega.

8
CONFESSION

Confession is one of the best tools to practise spirituality. It brings one closer to the self.

Confession: Yes I was involved in 'Public Indecency.' (Just two months before my marriage.)

We decided to meet near the Thane Lake. And Jab we met, we were on cloud nine. 'Aaj Main Upar Aasma Niche' types.

We were looking into each other's eyes. The experience was similar to that of an ophthalmologist looking into your eyes. I was looking for the next 'Date' in her eyes and she was looking for 'Commitment' in mine. It was then that I came to know that men are from Ambernath and women are from Dadar.

After some time, Hawaldar (Police Constable) entered the scene.

Constable: Ye Kya ho raha hai? Tumhala Ghar Nahi kaa?

The next time, I booked a room. And was anxiously waiting for her.

I received a call.

Wife: Sorry, Chhotoo, I forgot to tell you, today is my parent's anniversary. We are going out for dinner. Some other day. Sorry.

I went to a chemist shop to check if he can take 'it' back but he refused. He pointed to a board:

'Hum Becha hua 'MAAL' Wapas Nahi Lete.'

Cut to August 2015 (10 years after marriage).

I booked a room in farm stay house. We were so excited. I reached home. Now, I had to perform the most difficult task. Breaking the news to my mother.

Me to my mother: Aai ('mother' in Marathi), we are going out for a day will come back tomorrow. Food everything is ready. You have to adjust just for a day.

Mother (almost in tears): Chhotoo, how can I stay alone? Please don't leave me alone. It is scary.

I looked at my wife. And without bothering to ask her, Mama's boy decided to take his mother along.

In the farm stay,there were 3–4 couples. They partying till 3 am. Meanwhile, my wife, my son and my mother slept on a comfortable bed. While in the same room. I slept on the floor. (I had to pay INR 300 extra for the bed). Adding insult to injury, my son, mother, and wife were snoring in rhythm, as if they were singing some anthem.

This is the 'jeevan' of typical middle-class husband and wife. But why am I publishing this today?

As they say, 'Mauka Bhi Hai Aur Dastur Bhi Hai.'

9

What is Maya?

'What is Maya?' I typed this on Google and got several results. Then I saw one featuring Shah Rukh Khan. Curious to know what it was, I clicked on the link. It was 'Maya Memsaab,' the movie. Then I saw Deepa Sahi, the actress in the film and many links related to her. I clicked on the link and this continued for almost half an hour. Then I realized that I had first wanted to know the metaphysical reason for Maya… instead I was reading everything except the intended article.

This is 'Maya.'

This reminds me of famous song from Umraao Jaan:

'Justaju Jisaki Usako to Naa Paaya Hamne

Is Bahaane Dekhali Duniyaa Hamne.'

There is similar story in the life of sage Narada. Once, he asked Vishnu the same question, "What is Maya?" Vishnu said, "First fetch me some water then I will tell you." Narada went to a river to get the water. There he saw a beautiful girl. He proposed to her, they got married and they lived happily ever after.

Then one day, due to heavy rains, his house gets washed away and so does his family. Just as a log of wood is carried away by a current of water, Sage Narada is carried away by water. He reaches the shore of a river where he finds Vishnu waiting for him.

Vishnu: Narada, why did you take so long to fetch water?

Narada: My dear Lord, now I understand the meaning of Maya. This life is like a dream.

This reminds me of another line from Umraao Jaan, the same song:

'Zindagi Tujh ko To Bas Khwaab Me Dekha Humne

Justaju Jisaki Thi Usko To Naa Paaya Humne.'

10

Immortal World

I am neither a God-realized soul, nor a self-realized soul, but definitely a Life-realized soul. And one thing Life has taught me is that never ever become a follower, a devotee, or a fan of a mortal soul. The end result is always frustrating. It is not worth spending time and energy in defending or glorifying these mortal souls.

If we can't live without defending them, then one solution could be, to offer issue-based defence/support in their favour.

This world would be a better place to live in if more and more souls take to defending and glorifying the IMMORTAL.

CHAPTER 4

MOVIES

1

Move On

Bollywood has finally discovered its song on 'Divorce.'

"Move on, Move on, Move on…" from 'Tanu Weds Manu.'

But the lyrics of the song are frightening. The song is a gentle reminder to all the husbands (those who take their wives for granted, including me.)

'Naya Jahaan Hum Jab Bhi Basayenge

Koi Khuda Bhi Hum Dhoondh Ke Laayenge

Jo Mila Nahi Koi Us Qaabil

Hum Khud Hi Khuda Phir Ban Jaayenge

Move On, Move On, Move on…..

O Miya ….'

My wife enjoyed the movie very much. But after watching the movie, I definitely did not find her 'swagger' S…Y. It was scary. Her new found confidence was evident in her new caller tune. And you know what the caller tune is?

'Move on, Move On…'

2

Prince of Death

If you have four hours left in your 'Life,' account then go watch 'Piku' and 'Tanu Weds Manu.'

If you have just two hours left in the account then watch the first half of 'TWM' and the second half of Piku.

If you watch these movies, then I can guarantee you that the Prince of Death (read Yamraj) will give you a top-up in your 'Life' account.

If not top-up, then the Prince of Death will come riding on a Light Commercial Vehicle (LCV) instead of his official carrier (HCV).

And we all know what Kangana Ranaut (Kusum) is capable of. Only Kusum has the audacity to tell the Prince of Death .... "Woh dekh Kabutar"

Sujit Sarkar, Amitabh Bacchan, Deepika and Irfan deserve a standing ovation for the movie 'Piku.'

But the real star of the film is scriptwriter Juhi Chaturvedi. She deserves a standing ovation and a golden 'SINHAASAN.'

3

Asian Tigers

We had the distribution rights of the Raj Kapoor, Nutan starrer film 'Dil Hi To Hai.'

My proud mother, sister, brothers, cousins, maternal uncle and grandmother had gone to watch the afternoon show. When we reached the theatre, we saw the 'Housefull Show' board. Everyone felt so proud of that moment.

It was then my brother (young distributor) reached there. Actually, he was supposed to have booked the tickets but had forgotten.

Finally, the exhibitor arranged for some extra chairs. We watched the re-issue version of 'Dil Hi To Hai' with each song being cheered. Chilar being thrown at the screen. It was proud moment for my brothers and my family.

Such were the days. After my father's death, my brother looked after his film distribution business well.

But something happened afterwards. Now, in 2015 we are all scattered. My hugely talented brothers are doing regular 9–5 jobs. And I know that they are not enjoying it. But I am helpless, main kya kar sakta hu?"

What went wrong? We forgot the adage:'United we stand, divided we fall.'

That is why I always feel that India, Pakistan and China can become Asian Tigers. Perhaps they can learn from the Ghadge's experience.

4

'A' Certificate

This post is given an 'A' certificate. Children below 18 are not supposed to read this post. Waise they should not be on Facebook anyways.

Porn in India (In the no-Internet Era)

I was preparing for a history unit test. It was then that a friend of mine called.

Friend: Chhotoo, my parents have gone to attend a funeral. Let us watch 'Blue Film' today.

Me: What if they come back early?

Friend: No, it's confirmed they will return only in the evening. The body has not arrived as yet, it is still in hospital.

We went to a VCD shop and bought two VCDs. (1) Aawara (2) XXX rated BP movie. Within an hour, all my friends had ganged up to watch BP' at my friend's place.

First interruption.

Grocery wala came. We panicked thinking that the parents have arrived and we immediately put the 'Aawara' VCD on.

We could not watch the movie peacefully because:

'Zara Si Aahat Hoti Hai

To Dil Sochata Hai

Kahi Ye Wo To Nahi' (Read friend's mod/dad).

Our situation was similar to Zeenat Aman's in 'Satyam Shivam Sundaram.'

('Suni Jo Unaki

Aane Ki Aahat

Garib Khaana Chupaaya Hamne.')

Grocery wala: Sab items check kar lo. Baad me bolne ka nahi.

Friend: Abe Saalo, mute karke dekho yaar marvaoge kya?

Me: Without volume kya mazaa hai?

This is how we used to watch pornographic movies before the time of the internet.

Those were the days. Today's generation has got it easy, on hand held devices. Now that the porn sites have been banned, let them discover ways and means to watch such movies!

5

Single Screen Theatre vs. Multiplex

The other day I was watching 'Bahubali' with my wife. Within ten minutes my reaction was, "Oh, shit! I should have watched this movie in Hyderabad in a single screen theatre."

Watching a movie in a single screen theatre is altogether a different experience. Nowadays, whenever I watch movies in multiplexes, I somehow miss the frontbenchers. Without these frontbenchers, the movie is incomplete. They shout, clap, whistle, dance, throw money and make movie-watching a 'Paisa Vasool' (value-for-money) experience.

They would start whistling the moment the Censor Board Certificate appears on the screen. Then the close-up shots of the hero would make them go absolutely crazy.

I remember watching the Shammi Kapoor-Saira Banu Starrer movie 'Junglee' in Variety Theatre Nagpur. There was this song:

'Din Saara Guzaara Tore Anganaa

Ab Jaane De Mujhe More Sajana'

The moment Saira Banu/Shammi Kapoor would sing:

'Mere Yaar Shabba Khair

Mere Yaar Shabba Khair…'

The front benchers would go crazy, and start dancing, whistling… and we could not hear a single word of the dialogues. (We had the distribution rights of the movie.)

I still miss those moments during the interval.

I am dying to hear the sound of

'Trin Trin Trin –

Ae Cold Drink, Campa Cola, Gold Spot

Ae Garma Garam Samosa

Ae Cold drink… le Popcorn…'

Nothing can match the experience of watching a movie in a single screen theatre.

Whenever I watch a movie in a multiplex, I wonder where the front benchers have gone.

Have they stopped watching movies? I miss them. All I can say is:

'Koi lauta De Mere

Bite Hue Din….'

(Before leaving this mortal world I have a thousand wishes to be fulfilled. #400th wish: To watch a Rajanikant movie in Tamil Nadu. Will it get fulfilled? I have so many Tamil friends, Surendher will you not help fulfill this wish of your dear friend?)

6

Dashrath Manjhi

17th August is not an ordinary day. Why? Find out the reason in this post:

In the 70's, people used to sleep outside the theatre to get the first day, first show tickets of Amitabh-starrer movies. Such was the craze, such was the expectation.

There is a similar buzz/craze around the Nawazuddin Siddiqui starrer 'Manjhi-The Mountain Man.'

In recent times, I haven't seen such a craze/expectation from any other star or movie.

In Chapter 10 of the Bhagwad Gita, Krishna describes his opulence thus:

'Of the Ādityas I am Viṣṇu

Of the lights I am the radiant sun

Of the Maruts I am Marīci

And among the stars I am the moon

Of the Vedas I am the Sāma Veda

Of the demigods I am Indra the king of heaven

Of the senses I am the mind

And in living beings I am the living force [consciousness].

Of all the Rudras I am Lord Śiva,

Of the Yakṣas and Rākṣasas I am the Lord of wealth [Kuvera]

Of the Vasus I am fire [Agni], and of mountains I am Meru.'

Perhaps in the future, we will get to read that"

'Among the hard-working men I am DASHRATH MANJHI.'

'Gar Majhi saare saath mein gair ho Bhi jaayein

To khud hi to Patwaar Ban

Paar honge hum – Kinaare.

Jo Chhoti si har ik neher saagar Ban Bhi jaaye

koi Tinka Le ke haath mein dhoondh Lenge hum

kinaare. kinaare. Kinare.'

Today is Dashrath Manji's death anniversary.

I am eagerly waiting to watch the movie.

CHAPTER 5

INDO-PAK

1

Friendship Day

(And friendship knows no boundaries)

Indo-Pak Friendship (2030) Venue: FTII (Pune)

Students across the border are now taking interest in each other's culture, art, theatre, movies.

My son and his friend from Pakistan are studying in FTII Pune. They are working on an Indo-Pak joint venture.

Krish: 15 years ago, India-Pakistan friendship was unthinkable.But my father always used to tell my mother, "Wait, India and Pakistan will become friends. It is just a matter of time."

Krish (again): Here are my father's thoughts on the lines of 'Phir wahi Raat Hai' penned by Gulzaar and set to music by RD Burman.

Karni Hai Baat Re...

The song is about the 'Importance of dialogue between the two countries.'

Will publish in an hour.... I am struggling to type in Hindi fonts.

My wife is helping me to type the song.

करनी है बात रे

बात ही बात से सुलझा करेंगी उलझनें

कब तक यू लडतें रहें

कब तक यू तानें कसें

कब तक यू इक दुसरें के

खून के प्यासे बनें

गुत्थि ना सुलझे अभी तो

कोसेगी नई नसलें...1

गुजरा हुआ कल हमें

जब जब याद आयेगा

कारगिल हो या बांगलादेश

हमको भी याद आयेगा

पीछें है एक हादसा

आगे है एक रोशनी

तपती हुई धूप में

भीगे ये बरसात में

जान पर खेलकर

सीमा कि रक्षा करे

इनका भी तो संसार है

इनकी भी है उलझनें

इसीलिए करनी है बात रे...2

'Happy friendship day!'

2

Pati-Patni Aur Woh (India-Pakistan and J&K)

Husband and wife fought bitterly over the custody of their kids. Finally, in 1947, they decided to part ways. The son decided to stay with the husband and the daughter decided to stay with the wife.

The spouses fought with each other over the custody of their kids again and again. The wife always felt that the son was not happy with the father. She took the matter to court.

The kids wanted their parents talk to each other and involve them in their discussion.

Father's stated position always was and is, "No third party mediation. The matter will be mutually resolved by your mother and me. Tum abhi bacche ho (you are kid)."

On many occasions, when the husband and wife met, their kids hoped that the matter will get resolved. But alas!!!!!!!!!!!

Yesterday, the husband and wife met in a foreign country. They talked with each other for an hour. Both of them made a resolution: "Commitment to peace, and no hostility." Their chemistry was awesome. But there was no mention of kids in their one hour long discussion.

The kids were happy. Kids always love to see their parents meeting and talking to each other. But the kids were asking, "Can there be everlasting peace, without involving us?"

The kids are always in a state of anxiety. Their emotions can be summarized in these lines:

'Zara Si Border Par Halchal Hoti Hai

To Dil Sochta Hai

Ladenge Ye Phir To Nahi

Aur Zara Si Baatchit hoti hai

To Dil Sochta Hai

Banegi Shanti Abhi.'

3

Jammu and Kashmir

The ex-RAW chief, in a candid interview to Barkha Dutt said something very important:

"You cannot understand Kashmir without empathizing with it."

As Vajpayee once famously said, Kashmir should be seen from the 'Insaaniyat' angle.

But the warmongers who salivate at the prospect of a war with Pakistan, do not realize what the Kashmiris go through.

Their plight can be summarized on these lines (song from Haquequat):

'Zara Si Border Par Halchal Hoti Hai

To Dil Sochta Hai

Ladenge Ye Fir To Nahi.'

And when the two countries resume their dialogue, the feelings of Kashmiris can be summarized as:

'Zara Si Baatchit Hoti Hai

To Dil Sochata Hai

Banegi Shanti Abhi

Banegi Shanti Abhi.'

But the question is:

'Hai Ye Gar Bharat Ka Ang

To Use Dard Hota Nahi Kya?'

4

Indo-Pak Dialogue

Pakistan's National security advisor Saraj Aziz is going to visit India for talks with his counterpart tomorrow. Here is my advice to both of them:

Forget talks. Forget Hurriyat. Forget Kashmir. Forget terrorism.

Just go and watch 'Manjhi-The Mountain Man.' I am sure that at the end of the movie both of them will agree that:

"If a man with only a sledgehammer, chisel and a crowbar can single-handedly carve a road through a 300-foot mountain, then what stops the two nations from bridging the gap, forget their differences and bring about peace in the region?"

If politicians can't bring peace then people should take the initiative.

Don't leave diplomacy to the diplomats.

"IN Diplomats Ke Bharose Mat Baithiye

Ka Pataa Ye Diplomats Hamaare Bharose Baithe Hoge

Jab Tak Jodenge Nahi

Tab Tak Chhodenge Nahi."

5

Indo-Pak Talks Failed Yet Again

The two nations should continue to talk irrespective of hindrances.

Here are few lines on the importance of Indo-Pak dialogue on the lines of 'Waqt Ne Kiya Kya Hasin Sitam'– from 'Pyaasa.'

'Istemaal Hoga

Jab Nuclear Bomb

Hum Rahe Na Hum

Tum Rahoge Tum....

Kataleaam Se

Kuch Hua Nahi

Kataleaam Se

Kuch Hoga Nahi

Baat Baat Se

Baat Banati Hai

Har Mushkilon Ka

Hai Yahi To Hal

Istemaal Hoga.....

Ghaav Gahre Hai

Hai Yaadein Buri

Jo Hua Use

AB Bhula Bhi Do

Aage Badho,

Ab Gale Milo

Jab Milego To

Bhar Do Ye Zakham

Istemaal Hoga…..

Aane Waale Kal Ke

Sar Pe Chat Rahe

Aane Waala Kal

Naa Bhuka Rahe

Bhook Pyaas Ko

Pehle Jeet Lo

Mat Lagaon Dhan

Yu 'Defence' Mai

Istemaal Hoga…'

Aapka optimistic…

6

It's Time to Take a Stand

Chalte Chalte Mujhe Hindu Kah Gaya Tha

Soya Nahi Main To Kal Se

Jab Rahim Jal Raha Tha

Main Tamaasha Dekh Raha Tha

Mat Jalao Yaaro Mujhko

Dafnaao Yaaro Mujhko

Roe Ruh Jalte Jalte

Kyu Ram Rahim Ke Naam Par

Ye Jamaana Kat Raha Hai

Ye Jamaana Bat Raha Hai

Ye Jamaana Chat Raha Hai

RAM base Hai Tere Dil Me

Mat Nikalo Inke Jalse

7

Katti Diplomacy

My son (Krish) was desperately waiting for my nephew and niece to come this summer vacation. Finally, when they came, they spent a full week here. But whenever Krish would disagree with his cousins, he would not talk to them. 'Katti' became his favourite weapon and he would use it quite regularly. My wife said, "Krish, they are here for a week and you are wasting most of your time in fighting/not talking with them."

This reminds me of the song 'O, Dilbar, o dilbar jaaniyaa, Ruthane Manane me naa bite ye Jawaaniya…'

India's relations with her neighbours, especially with Pakistan, and Srilanka, is based on this 'Katti diplomacy.' Even a slight provocation makes our diplomats and foreign officials use this favourite weapon: "We will not talk until and unless …."

And looking back, this 'Katti diplomacy' did not produce any results. I think Narendra Modi has surprised many of us with his decision to invite all SAARC leaders, including the Pakistan PM.

Narendra Modiji, please ignore Jaylalitha's displeasure on your decision to invite Srilanka's president.

'Karni hai baat re, karni hai baat hi baat re

Baat hi baat se, suljha karegi uljhane...'

'So, Batti is the best diplomacy, when it comes to foreign policy.'

CHAPTER 6

SHORT STORIES

1

Indian Culture vs. Western Culture

Women wearing jeans, blame Western culture

Children eating noodles, blame Western culture

A few days ago, I was watching a movie 'Masaan.' There were hardly ten people (including my wife and me) watching the movie. But by the time the movie came to an end, there were hardly 4–5 people left.

Overseas, at the Cannes Film Festival, the film received a five-minute standing ovation when it ended.

Oh, standing ovation se yaad aaya.

'Wo to western culture hai.'

2

Sharing Love

Too much is said about giving and sharing love. But what about receiving love? This love deficit causes havoc in our life.

Sharing (love) without receiving it is a fraud/farce.

Always remember:

Pehle

Pyaar Lo Fir Pyaar Do.

3

'Male' Ego

My wife and I fought bitterly yesterday. But my anger is like water vapour,'Gone with the Wind.'

Today, I want to watch 'Bahubali' with my family.

Retaining my 'Male' ego how can I break this news to them?

(Ruthane Manane me naa bite ye kahaniya…)

'Bade Wafa Se Nibhayi Tumne

Hamaari Thodi Se Bewafaai…..'

4

Me and my Facebook

After spending quality time on Facebook, it's time to log off.

Me to Facebook: Din sara gujara tore angana

Ab jaane de mujhe more sajana

Mere Yaar Shabba khair

Mere Yaar Shabba Khair

Facebook: Aasan Hai Jaana Mehfil Se

O Kaise Jaaoge Nikalkar Dil Se

Mere Yaar Shabba Khair

I Mere Yaar Shabba Khair

Good night friends, and listen to this song from 'Junglee.'

5

EMI

Last Saturday, I had a telephonic conversation with a very dear friend of mine. We spoke for almost half an hour. But at the end of the conversation, she said, "Chhots, I do not know why, tum aajkal khul kar baat nahi karte. Haste bhi ho to dil se nahi haste, baat kya hai?"

I said, "I didn't tell you, I have bought a house. And since the time I have started paying EMI, aajkal mai EMI me hasta hu, EMI me bolta hu, Biwi se ladta /rtuthata/manata bhi hu to EMI main. Hope ye din bhi gujar jaayenge."

It's time to take life seriously, time to change gears. Don't know whether I will be able to play this new role.

'Muskurao To Dar Lagta Hai, Jaise Hoto Pe Karz Rakha Hai.'

6

LET'S DYE TOGETHER

My (dear) wife,

Today I found a white hair in my lunch box. Tumhaare baal kab safed ho gaye mujhe pata hi nahi chala. You didn't tell me.

For the last four years, people have been saying, "Chhotooji, ab bal ko colour laga do." But I was waiting for this day. There are many saloons which give discounts to couples.

We have spent ten years together, now let us DYE together.

Let us look young once again.

Ek duje ke liye.

7

Men Will Always be Men

My biwi is going to her maika tomorrow and she is as super-excited as I am. The reasons for her excitement are different though.

Yesterday she said, "Chhotoo, tumhe kal mujhe station chodne ki jaroorat nahi, main manage kar lungi. You take rest, since the last week has been very hectic for you." (The journey from my house to the station is nearly 80 kms.)

I said, "No no, chahe jo kuch bhi ho, main tumhe chodne jaroor aaonga, I want to spend every time, and every moment with you."

(The fact of the matter is, I want to make sure that she really leaves Bangalore so that I can relieve my bachelorhood.)

Moral of the story, men will always be men.

Happy Looooong Weekend.

CHAPTER 7

GENERAL

1

Nothing Religious About It

The movies of Shyam Benegal and Govind Nihlani have one thing in common. The music director – Vanraj Bhatia.

Vanraj Bhatia's body of work includes 'Manthan,' 'Discovery of India,' 'Tamas,' 'Drohkaal' and 'Junoon.'

So, when I came to know that he has set the verses of the Bhagwad Gita to music, I was desperate to listen to the work.

I reached Times Music (just opposite CST Mumbai) and found that the entire set comprising 6–7 cassettes was priced at around Rs. 300 +.

15 years ago, spending Rs. 300 on a music album was a luxury.

But, in the next two days, I received a bonus of Rs. 500. I took half-day leave and bought the Gita set. And I did not have patience to wait till I reached home. I started listening to it while travelling in the local train.

When I first heard this Gita album which was in operatic style, I could not check my emotions. Imagine in the crowded train, where I did not get place to sit, I was listening to the shlokas and was in tears.

One of the commuters offered me a place to sit.

Before quitting this mortal world, I have thousands of wishes to be fulfilled. One such wish is to see the Bhagwad Gita as a movie.

So, when I was watching 'Bahubali,' I thought that my dream #1, that is, a movie on the Bhagwad Gita is not a distant dream.

(Once when I was in Mumbai, I sought an appointment with Govind Nihlani. He agreed but I could not meet him as there was one urgent deliverable. But I have not given up yet.)

My friend Surendher has volunteered to take care of my wish #400. But who will fulfil my #1 wish?

My #2 wish is to meet Vanraj Bhatia. I bow down to the talent of this genius.

Take time to listen to this operatic rendition of the Gita verses. I recommend that you listen to it in a home theatre.

Don't download it. Purchase it from Times Music, and you will get a booklet of the verses with their meaning.

Whenever I feel depressed, I imagine myself as Arjuna on the battlefield of Kurukshetra and then I play this music. This is my anti-depressant. I just listened to it before I wrote this post.

2

BEAUTIFUL MIND

Yesterday, I discovered a friend of mine on Facebook. He was my classmate. We studied together till the seventh standard. Here is the conversation that took place last night.

Friend: By the way, your favourite teacher is also on Facebook.

Me: You mean to say, Sunita ma'am? (Name changed.)

Friend: Her Facebook id is ....

Me: You still remember her?

Friend: How can we forget her, Chhotoo? How can we forget that famous rather infamous incident involving you and the teacher?

FLASHBACK

My class teacher Sunita was beautiful. I used to like her very much.

But she was having an affair with our Maths teacher, Amar sir (name changed). One day, I caught them holding hands.

I was furious. I could not tolerate someone holding the hand of my favourite teacher.

That day, I went to washroom and wrote on the wall 'Sunita Loves Amar.' Someone did the 'chugli' and I was summoned by the principal.

Principal: Chhotoo, please ask your parents to come and meet me tomorrow. What you have done is very serious.

A month later, both Sunita ma'am and Amar sir entered the classroom to give us this news.

Amar: Sunita madam and I are going to get married. This is our invitation card.

After their honeymoon, when Sunita ma'am came back, I could not take my eyes off her. While she was teaching 'Fill in the blanks,' I was looking at her 'sindoor.' When she was teaching 'Match the following,' I was looking at her saree and matching bindi and bangles.

While she was writing on the blackboard and was saying something, all I could hear was the tinkling sound of the bangles.

It was around the same time that my brother decided to leave Nagpur and settle in the Mecca of film distribution – Amaravati.

It was during lunch time that I met both Sunita ma'am and Amar sir. They were having lunch together.

Me: Ma'am, I am leaving, this is my last week in school.

Sunita ma'am: In the middle of the semester? Anyways, best of luck.

Sunita ma'am (again): Bring your lunch box, we will have lunch together.

Me: I have already eaten ma'am.

Sunita ma'am: Okay, best of luck and take care.

That was the last time I saw my beautiful teacher.

'Mubarak Ho Tumhi Ke Tum

Kisi Ke Noor Ho Gaye.'

Kisi Ke Itna Paas Ho

Ke Humse Door Ho Gaye…

Ajeeb Daasta Hai …..'

My favourite teacher is just one click away. I visited her Facebook page. She is a writer now.

She looks even more beautiful today. I have sent her a friend request and it is still pending.

Will she accept my friend's request, or delete it?

Please pray for me.

3

Verdict on the Gay Marriage

After the landmark judgement of the Supreme Court in the US, legalizing gay marriage, the community worldwide must be feeling something similar to what Waheeda Rahman expressed in 'Guide':

'Kal Ke Andhero Se Nikal Ke

Dekha Hai Aankhe Malte Malte

Phool Hi Phool Zindagi Bahar Hai

Tai Kar Liya

AAJ PHIR JEENE KI TAMMANA HAI

AAJ PHIR MARNE KA IRRAADA HAI....'

And their counterparts in India should not lose heart. They should instead remember the famous saying:

'No force on earth can stop an idea whose time has come.'

And last but not the least, my appeal to all the homophobic:

'Feel the pain of the community who are deprived of the basic right to LOVE.'

4

Hindu Rashtra

It was my second job. I used to teach basic computers at a school, for classes from KG to ninth. Such was my relationship with the students that no one could differentiate between the student and the teacher. I used to crack jokes with them, have lunch with them… It was fun. On Monday, I used to have lunch with the sixth class students. Tuesday, it would be lunch with the seventh class students and Friday, with the eighth and ninth class students.

It was 6th December, the anniversary of the demolition of the Babri Masjid. I asked the students of the seventh class, "What do you think about the demolition? Don't you think that the Hindus are guilty?"

Students: Sir, they deserve it…

Me: They? Who?

Students: They sir, the Muslims.

Me: There are three Muslim students in this class, what do you think about them. Put yourselves in their shoes and then speak.

One of the students stood up.

Student: Sir, you don't know, in Mumbra, whenever the Pakistanis win a match, they burst crackers.

Me: What about these three students, do you think they burst crackers too, when Pakistan wins?

Student: Sir, according to Balasaheb Thackeray, there are good Muslims too. They can stay in India and others can go to Pakistan.

I was very disturbed by the response.

The next day, I was summoned by Principal of the school.

Principal: Mr. Ghadge, the Hindu-Muslim issue is a very sensitive one. You should not have raised this in class. I will not tolerate this again.

Me: Sir, what was my fault? I merely asked the question.

Principal: Whatever…

Me: Okay sir. Then I would like to resign.

Principal: You will have to give us a month's notice.

Me: Sir, I feel suffocated. I want to resign now.

Principal: Okay… then you will not get the salary for this month.

Me: I am fine with it.

It was 1:15 pm. The students of the ninth class were waiting for me.

Me: Students, I am sorry. I cannot have lunch with you today. Today is my last day of school. I have resigned.

Students: What?

At around 3 pm, I received a farewell card signed by students and staff.

For three months I was without a job.

20 years later, I am still the same Chhotoo. Not comfortable with the idea of a Hindu Rashtra. It is dangerous.

5

Despite Being Durga...

Our son participated in a skating competition and won the third prize. I came to know of it when he showed me the certificate. I was surprised to see my name on it – 'Krish Chhotoo Ghadge.' Actually, I would have loved to see 'Krish Mily Ghadge,' as my wife was the one who had spotted talent in him and had done all the hard work.

This summer, he participated in a month long football class conducted in a decathlon, Bangalore. She used to drive 50 km (from our residence to the venue and back) every day. I hardly attended one or two sessions. My wife took regular feedback from the coach. On the last day of the class, Krish received a letter of participation "This is to certify that Krish Chhotoo Ghadge ......" I was really embarrassed to see my name, again.

Despite being 'Durga' my wife was not appreciated for her effort. So, my dear wife, please consider this post as my letter of appreciation.

My (dear) wife, remember one thing in life:

'Har Kisi Ko Nahi Milta

Yahan Award Zindagi Me

Khush Naseeb Hai Wo

Jinko Hai 'Mily' Ye Bahar Zindagi Me.'

I dedicate this post to my father who was a huge fan of Indira Gandhi. Yesterday my father came in my dream and said, "My dear son, for Bangladesh (Mukti Bahini), Indira –BAI deserves all the credit."

Even Atal Bihari Vajpayee, despite being in the opposition, hailed her as an avatar of Goddess Durga.

'Durga ko bhulkar

Durga bas kahne waale ko award dena

Yeh Acchi Baat Nahi.'

Disclaimer: Mere Baat Ke Maane Do

Jise Apna Lage Wo Apna Lo

Jise Bura Lage Wo Jaane Do.....

6
Jab Tak Hai Jaan

Yamraj Productions: Jab Tak Hai Jaan

Yesterday, the messenger of death knocked at my door. I asked for the warrant. The messenger said:

"Check your sugar levels/BP."

Within a minute I developed itching sensations all over my body. My face and eyes began to swell. My wife called our family doctor who gave me some painkiller injections just an hour back. I suspected that the itching sensation was because of the injections administered earlier. But the doctor said that the reaction to the injections should have appeared earlier and not two hours later.

I told him that there was no point in arguing. I asked him what to do. So taking his instructions, we went to a 24*7 hospital. My wife drove me there.

By the time I reached the hospital, my condition went from bad to worse. I could barely walk a few steps when I fell unconscious in front of the hospital then my wife called up 4–5 people to help to take me inside the hospital.

My sugar levels/BP, etc. were low. Our family doctor also arrived. He was feeling guilty but was trying to prove that the reaction was not due to the injections administered earlier.

I told the doctor to relax. I said, "Jab Jab So Hota Hai Tab Tab So So Hota Hai."

During the journey to the hospital, I chanted the holy names of the God. Now I was calling out the names of the Lord loudly. At around 2'o clock, when everyone had gone to sleep, I was loudly crying/praying for help – where was my favourite Lord? Why did he not appear in person and help me. He helped the Pandavas on many occasions and we all know it. But today…

My wife was fast asleep. She was tired. I had a momentary thought: Was she my favourite God, my Krishna, My 'Parthasarathy' who drove me from home to the hospital?

My dear wife, I must say ke:

'Tujh Me Rab Dikhta Hai

Yaara Mai Kya Karu

Sad Pe Sar Jhukta Hai…'

The good news is that the next day evening I would be discharged from the hospital. But I would like to thank all the doctors, hospital staff and of course, the 'Woman of the Match,' my wife.

No wonder my nine-year-old son always says, "Darne Ki Kya Baat Jab Mily ho saath."

7

Frog in the Well

A few years earlier, my friend, mentor, guide… Parthasarathy Vallabhajosyula, along with his wife Rashmi Vallabhajosyula visited Mumbai and asked me if I was ready to work in Bangalore.

"No way," I told my wife, Mily Ghadge. I cannot imagine in my wildest of dreams, of leaving my brother and sister, I told her.

"Naa udane Ki Is Dafa Thaani

Parinde Ne Bhi Wafa Jaana

Andhero Ko Baho Me Lekar

Ujale Ne Ghar Basaya Hai."

But my wife played a trick. She said, "Chhotoo, do you know that Bangalore mai ISKCON hai." That very night I called up Partha and told him that I was ready to work in Bangalore!

Seven years have passed and I already love Bangalore.

And yesterday, we did pooja at our own house. I have now become a pucca Bangalorean.

I would like to thank all my friends in Bangalore – without your support it would not have been possible to continue my journey here.

I must thank my wife, for teaching me how to live in a city and LOVE it. Had it not been for her I would not have dare to step out of Ambernath.

She was instrumental in showing this 'frog in the well' that there is a life beyond Ambernath. "Lootero Ko Bagbaa banaye, Nasibo Ki Baat Hai."

This 'Shikayate' song from Lootera sums up my journey from Ambernath to Bangalore.

8

Special Women in My Life

Today's post is about a very special woman in my life. She is my childhood friend Javed Khan's mother.

I was studying in the fourth standard. My father had just left this mortal world. I did not go to school for 15 days as ceremonies related to the departed soul were needed to be completed.

After completing all the ceremonies, I resumed school. I was very happy to see all my friends and teachers. My friend Javed Khan was very happy to see me.

The next day, while we were playing during the recess, I saw Javed stop playing and run towards the school gate. His mother had come, along with her youngest daughter. She had come all the way to meet me.

Javed to me: Chhotoo, my mother has come to meet you.

Javed's mother to teachers: The last 20 days, when Javed could not see Chhotoo in school, every day he used to ask me, "Ammi where is Chhotoo? When will he come to school?" Yesterday, he told me that Chhotoo had come to school – he was so happy.

Teacher: Yes, he was also asking us almost every day, when Chhotoo would come to school.

Javed's mother to me: Beta, I came to know about your father's death. Don't you worry. Allah will take care of you and your family. Beta, khub man laga ke padhana. Apni Ammi ka Khayal Rakhna.

Mother to me (again): Beta, take care of your mother. Now your mother is your father.

I was too young to understand the seriousness of what she was saying.

Me: Ae Javed, let's play!

Teacher: Chhotoo, she has come to meet you and you want to play?

Mother: Koi baat nahi, baccha hai, abhi nahi khelega to kab khelega.

I still remember that the teacher did not allow me to play till Javed's mother and his younger sister had disappeared from sight.

That was the last time I saw her. Javed and I were together till the seventh standard. Then I left Nagpur and moved to Amaravati.

I had almost forgotten my friend Javed. I thought of Javed later, when the Babri Masjid was demolished. Afterwards, whenever Hindu-Muslim riots take place I think of my friend Javed and his mother.

Where is my friend Javed? Is he alive? Does he remember me? Where is Javed's family?

All these questions still bother me.

When the film 'Shahid' was released, I desperately wanted to see it. We got the tickets but the show was cancelled because only two tickets were sold. Finally we got the tickets in QCinemas Bangalore.

After watching 'Shahid,' I thought about my childhood friend Javed and his family. The 'Beparwah' song is my favourite from the movie.

'Khub Man Laga Ke Padhana, Apni Ammi Ka Khayal Rakhna.'

My dear friend Javed wherever you are, please convey this message to your mother. "I have not done badly in studies and I am taking care of my mother as promised."

Hope you and your family are safe.

I was in the third standard. In the Parent's Day function, I played the role of Adi Shankaracharya. I was wearing saffron clothes and chanting, "Bhaj Govindam Bhaj Govindam, Govindam Bhaj Mudha Mate." After the performance, Javed's mother appreciated me. She said, "Kitne pyaare lag rahe ho."

After the Babri Demolition, this is what I penned down and I dedicate these lines to Javed, especially his mother, who gave me my first lesson in secularism:

'Hindu Muslim se waada Ye Karle

Ke Tujh Par Aanch Naa Aaye Mere Hote

Hindu Apne Man Me Mandir Bana Le

Muslim Apne Man Me Masjid Bana Le

Ishwar Tere Yahi Base Hai Allah Yahan Re....'

'Hindu ki wahan laash padi hai

Muslim khoon se lathpath pada hai

Arey Baccha tu kyu rota hai

Teri Maa hai kaha Re

Hindu Muslim se waada karle...'

9

Presence of the Father

Telephonic conversation with my friend who stays in my birthplace, Nagpur. She is my school friend.

Friend: Chhots, sorry I could not reply to your emails. There is bad news.

Me: Whether the news is bad or good, that I will decide, now tell me.

Friend: Chhots, my father is no more.

Me: Oh, then it's a good news for him, but bad news for you.

Friend: Chhots, I cannot imagine life without my dad. He was my pillar of strength, friend, everything...

Friend (again): Chhots, how old were you when your father died?

Me: Quite young. 10-years-old...

Friend: How did you cope with the loss?

Me: Frankly speaking, I never felt his absence. I still remember him 24*7, literally. I still believe that he is still here, somewhere. I strongly feel his presence whenever I watch a movie. Then we discuss the minute details of the film.

Always remember this song, then, you will never feel your father's absence. This is my favourite. (My father used to look like Ashok Kumar.)

Friend: Which song?

Me: 'Rahe Naa Rahe Hum

Mehka Karenge

Banke Kali, Banke Saba

Bagel Wafa Mai.'

10

My Techie Friends

I dedicate this to my techie friends of Bangalore, Hyderabad and Pune.

The problem with tech cities like Bangalore, Hyderabad and Pune is that everyone here talks in tech language.

Yesterday, I was sitting in our garden gazing at the stars, rather, taking a FREQUENCY count of the stars. It was then I saw a married couple. They came too close to me to ignore. When the husband (a techie) saw me, he held his wife even closer/tighter, as if I was RAVAN about to snatch his wife from him.

But the conversation between them was interesting. Husband to wife: “Yeh jo Chand dekh rahi ho naa…” Wife: “Yes, I can clearly see it in your eyes.”

Husband: “Isme bhi SYNTAX ERROR hai (Daag hai). Aur woh 90th percentile tara hai na (star) usey kabhi akele nahi dekhna chahiye.”

Then he saw a Red Rose: “Must be 1000*400 Pixels, I am sure.”

The other day, an old lady (almost my age) came to my house, “Do you know how to Skype? My son from Australia wants to chat with me. Mujhe poti hui hai.”

I said, "Wow, poti! Congrats, kitne pounds ki hai?"

Lady: "3 MB ki, abhi abhi email se bheji hai ladke ne, evening ko Skype par LIVE dekhna hai."

Then I went to the hair cutting saloon where the barber said, "Sahab pura FORMAT karu ki Aadha."

I said, "Medium."

Barber: "Sahab Balon ka PARTITION KARU?"

Font size TIMES ROMAN RAKHU yaar.

(Then he showed the SLIDES HOW of my hair from all angles.)

A young lady (a neighbour) gave me a bunch of keys. "Waise I will come back before my hubby, but in case I am late, please give these keys to him. Please be careful. These are the only PRIMARY KEYS left with us. My hubby has just lost his SECONDARY KEY."

Husband to his newly married wife (Aankho me Aankhe dalkar): "Nowadays, I have noticed one thing..."

Wife: "Kya?"

Husband: "Nowadays tum meri MAA ke saath BINARY me baat karti ho – "Yes," "No.""

Wife: "Accha to tum kaunsi STRUCTURE QUERY LANGAUGE MAIN baat karte ho meri mummy papa se?"

And last but not the least, My Binary numbers (Wife(1), Son(0)), come back soon, itni dhoop mai fashion street me ghumna accha nahi hai."